Illustrations and Design© 2015 by Jim DeLapine

First Published 2015
Kids Education Publishing, LLC
Atlanta, Georgia 30338
www.kidseducationpublishing.com

ISBN 978-0-9864472-0-4
Library of Congress Control Number: 2015901138

Ordering Information:
Quantity sales. Special discounts are available on quantity purchases by corporations, associations, and others. For details, contact the publisher at the address above.
Orders by U.S. trade bookstores and wholesalers.
Please contact Ingram book company: Tel: 800.937.0152; or visit www.ingramcontent.com.

Printed in the United States of America by an FSC certified Facility.

Bluefish & the Three Rs Plan

KIDS EDUCATIONAL PUBLISHING

Some time ago,
Sara the blue fish had her dream come true.
A magician gave her a pair of wings so she could fly.
At first, Sara could not fly well at all,
but her faith in herself
gave her the strength to keep trying.

Over time, she learned to fly very well.
Sara was excited to fly to distant lands to explore.
She traveled around the globe,
and from time to time she went back to the sea.

Sara enjoyed learning
about the people's food, music, and languages.
However, seeing the world's beautiful landscape
was her favorite thing to do.

One day, Sara landed on the shore of a small town in Italy where she saw two little American-Italian boys named Lane and Nate who were playing on the swings.

Both boys were very smart and loved to participate in their community's fun activities and projects.

Shocked to see a flying fish,
Lane and Nate jumped off their swings.
"Hi, welcome to the neighborhood!" Lane waved his hand.

As she got closer to them,
Sara could see the surprised look in their eyes.
She smiled and introduced herself.
Then she shared her story about
how she came to have wings and learned how to fly.
Soon the little blue fish and the two little boys
were the best of friends.

As Sara looked around, she felt sad.

"What is wrong, Sara? Why do you look so sad?"

Nate asked.

"Seeing the trash on the ground and in the river

breaks my heart."

"Yes, it is very sad," Nate replied.
"We always wanted to live in a clean town.
Lane, myself, and the people in the community
have cleaned it many times.
However, the town gets dirty again very quickly.
No one knows how to solve the problem."

"When people throw garbage in the river, sea turtles,
fish, and other animals eat it.
They think it is food and they get sick," said Sara.

"Oh my goodness! I did not know that,"
Nate was shocked.
Lane looked into the river sadly.
"Sara, how can we solve the problem?"

"We need to explain to the people in your town that they can reuse the things they no longer need instead of throwing them away. This will cut back on the amount of trash," Sara replied.

Lane's face lit up. "Will you tell us what you mean?"

"Instead of throwing away glass jars,
you can use them to hold pencils, pens, or paintbrushes.

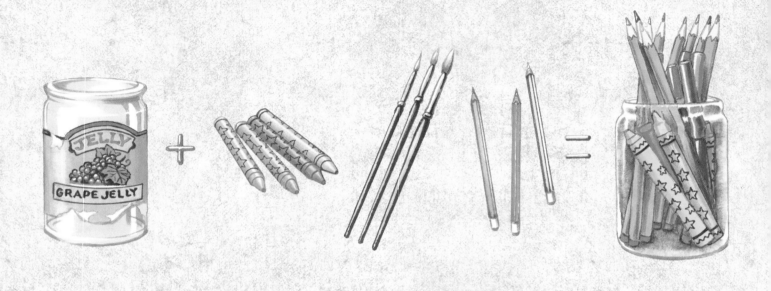

Empty plastic bottles
can be used to create flower pots.

Old cardboard boxes can be used to create handmade,
painted holiday ornaments or even gift boxes.

Instead of throwing away cans,
you can use them to create bird feeders.

Also... glass, cans, plastic, and paper,
can be taken to reprocessing plants
where they can be shredded into small pieces
that can be used to make new goods.

That is called the three Rs plan –
Reduce, Reuse, and Recycle."

Lane and Nate were very excited by the idea
and asked Sara to help them come up with a plan.

Sara flapped her wings.
"First, we need to find some bins
and ask all the people in the town to help us clean.
Then we should put the things that can be reused
into separate bins – one bin for paper,
another bin for plastic bottles,
and yet another for cardboard, and so on."

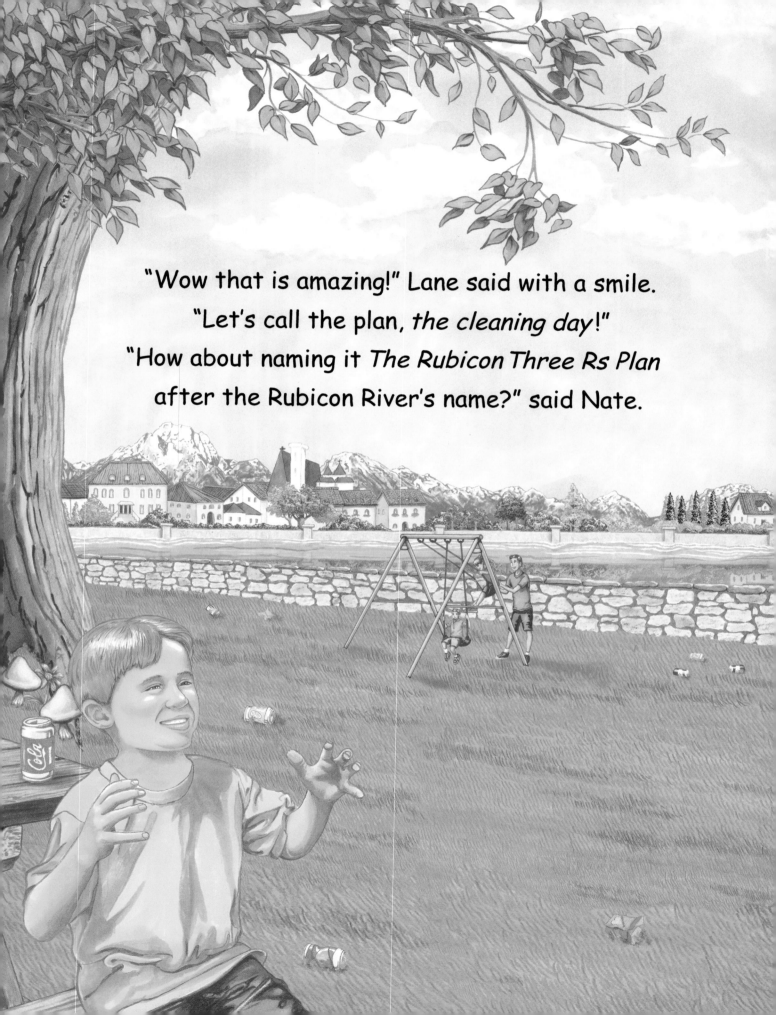

"Wow that is amazing!" Lane said with a smile.
"Let's call the plan, *the cleaning day!*"
"How about naming it *The Rubicon Three Rs Plan*
after the Rubicon River's name?" said Nate.

"Yes, yes, yes! That name is great!"
Lane said with excitement.

Thrilled by the name, Sara's eyes and mouth opened widely.
"Wow! 'Crossing the Rubicon' means
getting to a point of no return, which is exactly how we feel!
We will help solve the town's problem.
There's no turning back."

"Sara, how can we tell the people in the town?
It will take us days to go to each person's house?"
Lane frowned.

"I will get my flying friends to help us,"
said Sara, fluttering her wings.

"Oh, but wait.
We need to make some posters
and write invitation letters!" said Nate.

Lane looked worried. "How are we going to make posters? We have no thick paper to use."

Nate's eyes twinkled. "Let's think of something that we can reuse, as Sara has suggested."

Happily, Sara looked at them and smiled.

The two little boys sat under a tree to think.
They thought and thought,
yet none of their ideas were good ones.
They were starting to feel very glum indeed,
when a big grin spread across Lane's face.

"I've got it!
Let's take some of the cardboard boxes from the street
to use them for the posters!"

"What a wonderful idea!
Let's take a glass jar to hold our pencils,"
Nate replied with excitement.

The next day, Nate and Lane went
in search of cardboard boxes and glass jars.
They searched and searched
until they found what they wanted.

Then they wrote the invitation letters
and made beautiful colorful posters
that said:

In just a few hours, the sky above the town
was filled with birds carrying invitation letters
to all the people.

Lane's and Nate's friends joined in to help as well.
Of course, there was also Sara,
the little blue fish with wings,
who happily carried letters
asking for people's help.

The next morning,
Lane, Nate, Sara, the birds, and all the neighbors
collected and separated
the glass jars, plastic bottles, cardboard,
and cans from the streets and the river
and put each type in its special bin.

In the afternoon, the whole town became beautiful
and clean and the water in the river
started to become nice and clear.

Everyone cheered, sang, and danced.
Sara's bird friends chirped and warbled.
They all were so happy with what they had accomplished.

Thank you, Sara, for inspiring us
and for the great recycling idea!

Lane, Nate, and all the neighbors were so proud
of their new clean town and
promised Sara always to live by the rules of
The Rubicon Three Rs Plan.

CPSIA information can be obtained at www.ICGtesting.com
Printed in the USA
LVIW01n0400290415
436463LV00005B/12

9 780986 447204